Illustrated by Jacopo Camagni

withdrawn

First published in 2014
by Franklin Watts

Text © Jonny Zucker 2014
Illustrations by Jacopo Camagni © Franklin Watts 2014
Cover design by Peter Scoulding

Franklin Watts
338 Euston Road
London NW1 3BH

Franklin Watts Australia
Level 17/207 Kent Street
Sydney, NSW 2000

A CIP catalogue record for this book
is available from the British Library.

(pb) ISBN: 978 1 4451 2615 9
(ebook) ISBN: 978 1 4451 2619 7
(Library ebook) ISBN: 978 1 4451 2623 4

1 3 5 7 9 10 8 6 4 2

Printed in Great Britain by CPI Group (UK) Ltd, Croydon, CR0 4YY

Franklin Watts is a division of Hachette Children's Books,
an Hachette UK company.
www.hachette.co.uk

CONTENTS

CHAPTER 1
PLAYGROUND SHOUT

"I want to take that free kick!" shouted Gavin Mathers, striding across the playground.

"No way!" replied Leo Diamond, grabbing the ball and hugging it to his chest.

It was Friday lunchtime.

Ten vs ten on the playground tarmac.

Leo had just been tripped five yards outside the penalty area. There was no way he was going to let Gavin — the most annoying kid in his year — take the kick.

"Clear off, Gavin," said Leo's best friend Mac.

"Suit yourself," snapped Gavin, "but

I bet Leo misses!"

Leo placed the ball down on the ground and took a few steps back. Mike Young was the opposition's goalie. He was a good keeper, brave and a quick mover. Leo knew the free kick would have to be really good if he wanted to get it past Mike.

Taking a deep breath, Leo began his run-up, his eyes locked on the ball. He hit it hard with his instep and it moved at pace. But it shot forward in a straight line and whipped past the outside of Mike's right goalpost.

Leo groaned.

"What did I tell you?" shouted Gavin. "I should have taken it!"

Leo felt anger rising up in his chest, but Mac put a hand on his shoulder.

"Ignore him," said Mac. "Your free kick was way better than anything he could have done."

"Thanks," nodded Leo, calming down a bit. "But I wish I could have curled it. That way it might have nudged just inside the post."

"If only Mr Lawson could spend some more time training us rather than working with the older kids," sighed Mac.

Mr Lawson was an excellent football coach. He was supposed to be in charge of all the school teams, including the one that Leo and Mac played in. But they'd hardly seen him this term.

Instead they'd had Mr Cross, who was an OK guy, but he didn't have even the most basic of the FA coaching badges.

The bell rang for the end of lunch break and the football match ended abruptly. Leo picked up the ball and dropped it into his rucksack.

If only I could find someone to train me in the art of taking the perfect free kick, he thought, as he and Mac headed back inside the building.

* * * * * * * * * * * * * * * * * *

"How was school?" asked Mum when Leo got back to the flat at the end of the day. He felt like telling her about the free-kick incident with Gavin, but she had enough stresses to contend with at the minute.

So he gave his standard reply, "Fine."

Leo wished his dad was around.
When he'd been living with them, Dad
had regularly taken Leo down to the
local park for kickabouts and shooting
practice. But Dad was long gone,
married with two new kids and living
a couple of hundred miles away. And
though Mum was really encouraging
about Leo's football, she thought
Bolton Wanderers was a holiday
company.

"I'm doing spaghetti for supper,"
smiled Mum, standing in the kitchen
doorway, drying a bowl with a tea
towel. "Fancy giving me a hand with
the sauce? I need a vegetable chopper."

"Sure," nodded Leo, "but I'm going

to go on the laptop first for a bit."

"Of course," grinned Mum, "you can't separate a boy from his computer for too long, can you?"

Leo went to his bedroom, chucked his school bag onto his bed and booted up his laptop. Maybe he could find some free-kick inspiration on the Internet. He immediately went onto YouTube and found a link to the "World's Greatest Ever Free Kicks".

He flicked a key and the video montage began.

Here was Steven Gerrard's power smash for Liverpool vs Aston Villa in 2007. There was Cristiano Ronaldo's incredible dipping twenty-five yarder for Manchester United against Portsmouth in 2008. And number one was the legendary Brazilian left-back, Roberto Carlos — a swerving piledriver for Brazil vs France in 1997.

For this piece of free-kick magic, Carlos took a long run-up and smashed the ball with the outside of his left boot. It flew forwards, looking like it was going to go fairly wide of the left post. But at the last second it curled spectacularly inwards and whipped into the net. Incredible!

In Leo's dreams he was the free-kick master. He was Roberto Carlos and Steven Gerrard and Cristiano Ronaldo all wrapped into one player. And although he was pretty sure he would never be as good as any of those three, at least he could dream.

CHAPTER 2
THE MYSTERY DOOR

Leo was up early on Saturday morning.
After snatching a quick breakfast he
caught a bus into town. Excitement
bubbled in his body. He was going to
the country's newest attraction — the
21st Century Football Museum. He'd
been on the opening day with Mac, but
the queue had stretched so far they
hadn't managed to get inside. He'd
decided after watching the free-kick
videos that if his skills were going to
improve, it wasn't just YouTube he'd
need. He'd have to find out as much as
he could about the world's best free-
kick masters — how and where they
learned their skills, the secrets of their

techniques. And the Football Museum seemed like a good place to start. Mac was busy helping his dad, so today Leo had come on his own.

The queue was a lot smaller than it had been on Leo's first visit, but it was still quite long. He was about to sigh with disappointment when something caught his eye. There was a white

door in a passageway at the side of the building.

And it was open.

Leo looked around. No one else in the queue seemed to have noticed the door and there didn't seem to be any museum staff or security guards anywhere near it. He waited a few seconds, but then curiosity overpowered him. He slunk down the passageway to take a closer look. Stuck to the door was a handwritten sign:

STEP THIS WAY FOR THE PERFECT FREE KICK.

Leo gulped in shock and quickly spun round. Was this Mac's idea of a joke? Had his best friend set him up after hearing him going on about free kicks? Or was this a Gavin Mathers wind-up? Something designed to make Leo look stupid? But there was no sign of Mac or Gavin anywhere. Maybe it was just a coincidence, a pretty bizarre one, but just a coincidence.

Should he go in this way and find out what the sign was talking about? Would he get into trouble if he did? And if he went through would it really lead him to the perfect free kick, whatever that meant? Leo mulled things over for a few moments and then decided to go for it. Admission was free anyway so he wouldn't be denying the place the price of an entry ticket.

He stepped inside and found himself in a dim passageway that opened out onto a long corridor with whitewashed walls. He turned right and after a short distance came to a green door on the left. It had a pale, flashing light above it. As far as he could see, there were no other doors in the corridor.

Leo looked over his shoulder to check he was alone, then slowly turned the door handle and entered the room. The place was completely bathed in darkness apart from a single, powerful ceiling spotlight. This shone down on a glass case that contained an incredibly lifelike wax model of David Beckham. There he was: hair shaved, stubble on his cheeks, proudly wearing a white

England number 7 shirt and a captain's armband. Leo slowly walked over to the case. The model Beckham stared out of the case, unmoving and with a look of determination frozen on his face.

A plaque at the front of the glass gave some details of Beckham's career:

England caps – 115

England goals – 17

Trophies won include:
6 Premier League titles,
2 FA Cups and 1 Champions
League Title.

Clubs: Manchester United,
Preston North End (loan),
Real Madrid, L.A. Galaxy, A.C. Milan
(2 loan spells), Paris St-Germain

Leo read these stats in awe. How many players could claim that sort of record? He was about to turn around and investigate why there were no other lights on in the room, when a fierce and noisy gust of wind suddenly started billowing around him. In shock, he turned to see where it was coming from. But the force of it had grown so powerful that he had to close his eyes for a few seconds.

The wind swirled violently around him and then in a flash it was gone as quickly as it had started.

Leo slowly opened his eyes.

To his amazement, he was no longer inside the museum. Instead, he was standing in a park, surrounded on three sides by red-brick houses. Where was the dark room? And the glass case? How on earth had he got here?

But these new surroundings were nothing compared to the figure that was standing just a few paces in front of him.

"I must be dreaming!" mouthed Leo.

"You're not dreaming," smiled the figure.

It was David Beckham!

CHAPTER 3
THE REAL THING

David Beckham.

Not the wax model from behind the glass case in the museum.

Not a lookalike.

The real-life, bona fide David Beckham. Wearing a black tracksuit, with a blue duffel bag slung over his shoulder.

"All right?" said Beckham.

"I...I...I don't get it," gasped Leo, his mouth hanging open. "It's you, isn't it?"

Beckham nodded.

"But...but what about the museum, where's it gone?" asked Leo.

"Don't worry about that," said

Beckham. "Let's just focus on the fact that you want to become a free-kick master."

"Am I dreaming?" asked Leo.

"Absolutely not," replied Beckham.

Leo could feel his body reeling in shock. How did a world superstar like David Beckham know anything about him, a normal kid in a normal school living in a normal street? How come he knew about Leo's search for the perfect free kick? And whatever Beckham said about this not being a dream, it still might be one...

"Welcome to Leytonstone, East London," smiled Beckham. "This is the park near where I grew up."

"You practised here?" mouthed Leo.

"Absolutely," nodded Beckham.

"This was my field of dreams. I must have taken hundreds of thousands of free kicks here. I'd come by myself after school, put a ball on the ground and aim at the wire meshing of that community hut over there."

Leo turned round and saw the hut.

"When my dad got home from work he'd join me and we'd go over to those goalposts. Dad would stand between the posts and me, and force me to bend the ball round him. Time and time again we did that. It became like second nature to me. The other people in the park, walking their dogs or stretching their legs must have thought we were totally crazy!"

"Did you come here at weekends?" asked Leo.

"Of course!" laughed Beckham. "I spent whole days here with my dad. When the sun went down we'd carry on, playing by the lights coming out of the houses surrounding the park."

Leo was mesmerised.

"I'd heard that the greatest players of the past spent massive chunks of their childhoods improving their skills," said Beckham. "I wanted to really go for it — to be like them."

"That's just like me!" cried Leo. "I've been looking at the best free-kick takers of all time! I want to be like them!"

"That's good to hear," nodded Beckham.

"But I'm nowhere near as good as you were as a kid," said Leo, suddenly feeling downhearted.

"Forget about anything that's happened in the past," smiled Beckham. "This is where your free-kick journey begins. You've got the potential to be a free-kick pro! I'm going to show you a few things."

He tipped up the blue duffel bag and six white footballs fell onto the ground.

"What?" said Leo in shock, "you're going to train me?" His mind reeled at this incredible prospect.

"That's the idea," nodded Beckham, "come on."

Between them, they dribbled the balls to a spot about twenty yards from the two white goalposts.

"OK," said Beckham. "Are you ready?"

Leo felt his whole body zinging with

energy. He'd never been more ready
for anything!

CHAPTER 4
POSITION, BOOT WRAP, POWER

"My favourite positions for free kicks are about fifteen to twenty yards out," explained Beckham. "Anywhere from a central point to about twelve yards to the left of the goal. These are perfect spots for right-footed players like me."

"I'm right-footed too," said Leo.

"I know," replied Beckham.

Leo had no idea how Beckham knew which was his shooting foot — and he was getting more freaked out by the second — but he forced himself to concentrate and calm down a bit. Even if this was a dream, it wasn't every day you got coached in free-kick taking by one of the game's great masters.

"There are three aspects to taking a good free kick," said Beckham. "The first is the position of your run in relation to the ball. I favour approaching the ball from the left, again, because I'm right-footed."

He and Leo moved a few steps to their left.

"Your exact angle of approach will determine the ball's direction. If you want to hit it to the far right of the goal — by right I mean right from where you're standing, not right from the goalie's point of view — you'll need to approach from further to the left. From this new position you won't have enough space to make it curl to the far left of the goal. If you want to do that you'll have to move right a bit and take

your run from there."

Leo went over these positions in his mind.

"The second part is the way your foot hits the ball. The idea is to hit it with your instep and wrap your foot around the ball. This is how you get that curling motion. Remember, the opposing team will have made a defensive wall to block your strike. You have to curl your shot past them."

"Cool," nodded Leo.

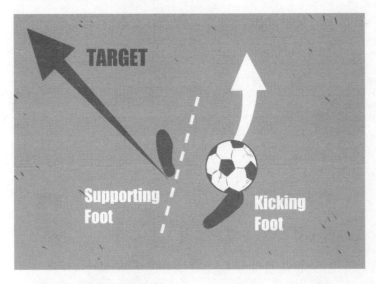

Beckham lined up a couple of balls and hit them with his boot-wrapping technique. The first he hit from further to the left. This one went screaming into the top right-hand corner of the net. The second he hit from further to the right and this curled majestically into the goal's top left corner.

"Wow!" said Leo.

"Your turn," said Beckham.

Leo gulped.

Beckham lined up four balls. "Mix them up, Leo. Send some to the right and some to the left."

Leo took quite a few steps to the left and hit the ball. It was a weak shot and missed the right post by quite some way. His second went the same way. For the third he moved a bit further to the right and smacked the ball. It cleared the bar by some yards. His fourth rolled slowly and stopped short of the goal.

"I guess I haven't got it," sighed Leo

as he and Beckham went to gather up
the balls.

"Don't be ridiculous!" scolded
Beckham. "Think how many kicks I had
to take before I was half decent."

"I suppose so," nodded Leo.

"The third thing to remember," said
Beckham, when they were back in front
of the goal, "is power. How hard you
hit the ball will define how fast it goes.
Hit it too hard and it will fly wide or
too high. Hit it too softly and a player
in the wall will head it away or the
keeper will grab it easily. You have to
strike the exact balance."

He smacked a ball with incredible
force. It flew over the posts. He hit the
next one with reduced power. It went
between the posts.

"Off you go," nodded Beckham, trotting to a spot between Leo and the posts just like his father had done for him all those years ago.

Following this, Leo experimented with angle of run, boot-wrap technique and power of shot. He took six, ran to get the balls and took another six. Beckham was constantly shouting out instructions, moving Leo left or right

and demonstrating some more of his trademark tricks.

An hour and a half and several hundred free kicks later, Leo was finally beginning to get the hang of it. He always focused on Beckham's three rules — position, boot-wrap and power.

"Nice one!" grinned Beckham as Leo sent a powerful drive curling round him and into the top right-hand corner of the goal. It was the sixth ball, so Leo scampered off to reclaim all six. As he ran he heard Beckham shout: "At this rate, you'll be seeing me again!"

But when Leo picked up the first couple of balls and turned round, he found himself completely alone in the park. All signs of his free-kick mentor — David Beckham — had vanished.

CHAPTER 5
NOT PITCH PERFECT

Before Leo could begin searching
for Beckham, a massive gust of wind
encircled him. His eyes shut tight
and when the wind evaporated Leo
was back in the museum room. This
time there were absolutely no lights
on. Leo could hear approaching feet
somewhere in the distance so he ran
out into the corridor. He retraced his
footsteps, exited the building through
the strange white door and hurried
away from the museum.

   As he walked to the bus stop he
debated with himself about whether
the training session with Beckham
had been real or imagined. Had he

somehow fallen asleep and dreamt it all? Or had it genuinely happened? He knew that if it was real, something quite unbelievable had just taken place. But if that was the case how had it happened, and who, if anyone, was behind it?

* * * * * * * * * * * * * * * * * *

"You're back early," said his mum.

"I'm just popping out to the Rec for a kickabout," replied Leo.

"How was the Football Museum?"

"Er...the queue was too long. I'll go back another time."

Leo's mum gave him a funny look. "But you were really excited about getting in this time," she pointed out. "It's not like you to give up just because there's a bit of a queue."

"It's no big deal," he smiled, "I'll go back another time."

The Rec was an old piece of open land behind the houses on Leo's street. No one really used it much, but Leo had cleared a large patch of weeds in the summer and now it was his own private football pitch. If you ignored the old Coke cans and soggy piles of yellowing newspapers, it could easily pass for Wembley Stadium.

In the past when Leo had come out here, he'd practised his keepy-uppies, done some running around and whacked the ball about, chasing it over the rough ground. Forget that. Now he had a purpose. He didn't know why it had happened, and he didn't know how it had happened, but he had just been trained in the art of free-kick taking by David Beckham. He wasn't going to waste a second.

Leo walked over to a large crumbling grey brick wall. This would be his goal. He looked around and found three old dustbins lying on top of each other. One by one he carried these over and placed them in a row about twelve yards in front of the makeshift goal. The bins were a defensive wall. It was round them that he needed to curl the ball.

With Beckham he'd had six balls. Now he only had two: a decent red leather one and a plastic black-and-white one he'd found on the Rec.

Position, boot-wrap, power.

Leo placed the balls down, stepped back a few paces and ran. The ball knocked over two of the dustbins. He stood the bins up and took another kick. This one missed the bins, but went wide of the goal.

And so it went on.

Shot after shot after shot.

Leo knew that if he practised now, the annoying Gavin Mathers could shout all he liked. Leo would prove to both Gavin and himself that he could take a good free kick.

CHAPTER 6
THE JOURNEY

There was a playground game on
Monday lunchtime. Leo had stayed out
on the Rec for the whole of Saturday
and most of Sunday. His free kicks
were getting better, but they weren't
brilliant yet. How long was it going to
take him to become a master?

Once again, Leo and Mac were on
Gavin Mathers's side, with Mike Young
in the opposition goal. But this time
it was Gavin who got fouled just
outside the opposing penalty area.
Leo was certain he'd already made
some improvements with his free-kick
technique, and he was tempted to
snatch the ball.

But he didn't feel confident, so he hung back and let Gavin have it.

"After your disaster last week," said Gavin smugly, "it's time for you to watch a proper free kick being taken."

"Be my guest," replied Leo.

"Stop talking," snapped Mike Young, "and get on with the kick."

Gavin took a really long run-up and hit the ball with his right foot. It was a decent effort, with power and direction. But it wasn't good enough and Mike pushed it over the bar with his fingertips.

"What was that about a proper free kick?" asked Leo.

Gavin scowled and stomped away.

* * * * * * * * * * * * * * * * * *

On Monday after school Leo spent three hours at the Rec, practising and practising his free kicks. He did the same on Tuesday and Wednesday, and was finally beginning to feel that he was turning into a decent free-kick taker.

On Thursday Leo planned to do the same and was eager to get home as quickly as possible after school. So he took a short cut down a side street leading to the High Road. He stopped when he saw a worn poster on a wall. It was an old advert for some football boots worn by David Beckham.

As Leo stared up at the poster and smiled when he remembered his training session, a massive blast of wind rushed down the street towards him. He was blinded for a moment and held his hand over his eyes. When the wind abruptly died down he opened his eyes. Leo wasn't in the street any more. He wasn't even in the park in Leytonstone.

He was inside a massive, noisy football stadium.

CHAPTER 7
ENGLAND EXPECTS

Leo looked around in shock. He was standing on the touchline of a ground he instantly recognised. It was Old Trafford — home of Manchester United.

There was an England game taking place on the pitch. Leo could see Beckham along with a few other

players he'd read about; there was the striker Teddy Sheringham, the goalie Nigel Martyn and the centre-backs Rio Ferdinand and Martin Keown.

It was a match from the past, but he couldn't quite place it.

"What game is this?" he asked a ball boy.

The ball boy looked straight through him and said nothing. Leo realised the ball boy couldn't see him. Being trained by Beckham in the park was completely incredible. But this was on another planet! This was a major international match and Leo was on the touchline, seemingly invisible!

Just then, the ball flew off the opposite side of the pitch and something totally amazing happened.

David Beckham, number seven, England captain, stepped out of the game — literally — leaving an outline of his body behind. He ran over towards Leo, while his outline stayed on the pitch, motionless.

"I told you we'd be meeting again," grinned Beckham as he reached the touchline and then patted Leo on the shoulder.

"I don't get it," said Leo, "when is this?"

"It's the sixth of October 2001," said Beckham. "England vs Greece in a World Cup qualifying game. Greece scored first, Teddy Sheringham came on and equalised for us, but then Greece scored again. It's 2–1 to Greece."

"Is it bad if England lose?" asked Leo.

"Bad?" said Beckham. "It's a disaster! Germany and Finland are drawing in the other group game. If we don't get an equaliser, England won't qualify for the 2002 World Cup Finals in Japan and South Korea!"

"So why am I here?" asked Leo.

"I thought I'd throw you in at the deep end," smiled Beckham, pointing to his outline, standing there, motionless on the pitch. "There are only three minutes of added time left."

"Are you crazy?" gasped Leo.

"I've never been more serious," said Beckham. "We've just got a free kick. Now get out there and take it!"

Leo stood rooted to the spot.

"Go on!" urged Beckham. "Move!"

Leo was still frozen to the spot, so

Beckham gave him a nudge on the shoulder. In a trance, Leo found himself running onto the Old Trafford pitch and slipping into Beckham's outline.

"No one will see you!" shouted Beckham after him. "But it is down to you what happens next!"

Leo stood over the ball, his body pulsing with fear and amazement.

"Get on with the free kick, Becks!" yelled Sheringham from inside the penalty area. "Time's running out!"

CHAPTER 8
THE TEST

The free kick was about ten yards inside the Greek half. Leo had to force himself to accept that this was really happening. He was actually about to take a crucial free kick for the England national team in a game of massive importance. To all intents and purposes, at this moment he was David Beckham.

It wasn't a shooting opportunity, so Leo floated the ball goalwards, watching it arc into the box. The Greek goalie caught it. It wasn't the best kick ever but it had been powerful enough and well directed enough, and he hadn't disgraced himself, or Beckham.

The ball was thrown out and passed between a couple of Greece players. Leo backtracked, hoping to see something of the ball, but it made its way back to Martyn in the England goal.

"Two minutes left!" called England's Swedish coach, Sven-Göran Eriksson.

Martyn quickly dribbled the ball out of his area, fully aware that England were on the verge of a total nightmare result. Looking up he punted a long hopeful ball towards the Greek penalty area. Sheringham jumped for it and got a slight nudge in the back from the Greece defender, Konstantinidis. It wasn't really a foul, but the ref blew anyway.

Free kick!

Ten yards outside the penalty area.

Almost completely central.

Leo grabbed the ball, rolled it in his hands and placed it carefully on the ground.

"Let me take it," said Sheringham, standing close to Leo's left. "It's my range. I've already scored once. I can do it again."

A part of Leo wanted to let Sheringham take the kick. But then Leo remembered the coaching he'd had from Beckham, and all of the practice he'd put in.

"No," said Leo firmly, "it's mine. I know what I'm doing."

CHAPTER 9
THE FREE-KICK MASTER

Sheringham shrugged his shoulders and backed away a few paces.

The tension inside Old Trafford was incredible. It felt like every England fan was holding their breath, waiting for Leo to stride forwards.

Everything Beckham had told him came to the front of his brain.

Position, boot-wrap, power.

Leo took a few steps back and placed his hands on his hips. If he scored he'd be a hero. If he missed...well, it wasn't worth thinking about. Yes he'd somehow travelled back in time and yes, he was inhabiting David Beckham's body, but none of that mattered at this second. He was out here on the Old Trafford pitch and he was about to take this free kick. Never had he felt this much pressure before. It made the playground games feel like a little kid's tea party. The hopes of an entire country rested on his shoulders.

Position, boot-wrap, power.

His arms were swinging at his sides, his stomach pumping with adrenaline.

And then he was moving.

One, two, three, four, five, six steps. He swung his leg and hit the ball on the sweet spot of his right boot, following through to give the kick that curling, arcing quality.

Round the Greek wall it flew, past the outstretched arms of the goalkeeper and into the top corner of the net.

GOAL!!!

Leo had scored with an inch-perfect Beckham-style free kick. Taught by the master. Scored like the master!

He ran to the England fans on the

left of the goal, leaped into the air and punched out his right fist as Emile Heskey and the rest of the team mobbed him.

"You're a hero, Becks!"

"Incredible, Becks!" his team-mates yelled at him.

ENGLAND 2 — GREECE 2. If England could hold on for the next minute or so they would be on the plane to the finals next summer!

When the other players released him, Leo ran back towards the centre circle for the Greece kickoff. It was then that he spotted Beckham on the touchline applauding him and motioning for him to come over.

Leo quickly ran to the touchline.

"YOU DID IT!" shouted Beckham, slapping Leo on the back. Leo quickly stepped out of Beckham's outline and Beckham slipped back in.

"It was a beautiful free kick," grinned Beckham, "almost as good as one of mine!" And with that, Beckham ran back onto the pitch, clapping his players and yelling at them to keep up their concentration.

Leo stood on the touchline, invisible to everyone in the stadium apart from Beckham, but glowing with pride at the sheer force and placement of his free kick. As the referee blew his whistle for full time and the stadium erupted, Leo felt the ferocious wind hitting his face. A second later he was back on the street looking up at the Beckham poster.

CHAPTER 10
THE FREE-KICK PRO

It was lunchtime the following day. Again, Gavin was on Leo and Mac's team. Ten minutes into the game Leo was running down the left half of the pitch, when an opposing defender stuck out a leg and tripped him.

"Free kick!" shouted Leo.

Everyone nodded.

The kick was twenty yards out, ten yards to the left of the goal.

A perfect spot.

"I'll take it," said Gavin, hurrying over and trying to nudge Leo out of the way.

"Erm, let's not forget you had your last one saved," Mac reminded him.

Gavin huffed and folded his arms. "At least it was on target, unlike your latest effort," he whined.

"I've put in a bit of free-kick training time since then," replied Leo. "I've got a better idea of what I'm doing now."

"Yeah, right," said Gavin sourly, "I'll believe that when I see it."

Mac gave Leo a funny look, but Leo winked at him and dropped the ball onto the tarmac. He trapped it with the sole of his left trainer.

Leo took six steps back, placed his hands on his hips and took a series of deep breaths.

This was his playground moment.

Position, boot-wrap, power.

He remembered Beckham's words of advice. Following them had worked out pretty well so far. And besides, after Old Trafford this should surely be a bit more straightforward. But the presence of Gavin so close made the nerves spiral up inside Leo. If he put this one past Mike, maybe Gavin would stop wanting to take every free kick and constantly questioning Leo's ability.

"Well get on with it!" moaned Gavin.

Leo looked at Mike in goal, and then at the ball.

And then he started his run-up.

Six equal steps towards the ball and then his leg was pulling back and smashing forwards. His instep made a good contact as his foot wrapped around the ball. Off sailed the ball with Leo's leg following through.

Every player stared as the ball

flew through the air. It looked like it might go wide to the right but curled beautifully to the left and smashed past Mike's desperate lunge, into the goal.

GOAL!

Leo wheeled away and punched the air to a huge bank of imaginary fans.

"That was BRILLIANT!" grinned Mac, racing after Leo and jumping on his back.

Gavin stood frozen to the spot, his mouth hanging open in stunned shock. Finally he managed to find his voice.

"Who do you think you are?" he shouted. "David Beckham?"

Leo could only laugh as he ran back to his own half and got ready for the kickoff.

FOOTBALL STAR POWER

There are four books to collect!

978 1 4451 2615 9 pb   978 1 4451 2619 7 ebook

EDGE **Free-kick Pro**
Jonny Zucker

978 1 4451 2616 6 pb   978 1 4451 2620 3 ebook

EDGE **Demon Dribbler**
Jonny Zucker

978 1 4451 2617 3 pb   978 1 4451 2621 0 ebook

EDGE **Driving Force**
Jonny Zucker

978 1 4451 2618 0 pb   978 1 4451 2622 7 ebook

Hottest Shot
Jonny Zucker